INVASIVE SPECIES

FERAL PIGS

by Alicia Z. Klepeis

pogo

Ideas for Parents and Teachers

Pogo Books let children practice reading informational text while introducing them to nonfiction features such as headings, labels, sidebars, maps, and diagrams, as well as a table of contents, glossary, and index.

Carefully leveled text with a strong photo match offers early fluent readers the support they need to succeed.

Before Reading

- "Walk" through the book and point out the various nonfiction features. Ask the student what purpose each feature serves.
- Look at the glossary together. Read and discuss the words.

Read the Book

- Have the child read the book independently.
- Invite him or her to list questions that arise from reading.

After Reading

- Discuss the child's questions. Talk about how he or she might find answers to those questions.
- Prompt the child to think more. Ask: Feral pigs have a great sense of smell. Can you name other animals that are super sniffers?

Pogo Books are published by Jump!
5357 Penn Avenue South
Minneapolis, MN 55419
www.jumplibrary.com

Library of Congress Cataloging-in-Publication Data

Names: Klepeis, Alicia, 1971- author.
Title: Feral pigs / by Alicia Z. Klepeis.
Description: Minneapolis: Jump!, Inc., [2023]
Series: Invasive species | Includes index.
Audience: Ages 7-10
Identifiers: LCCN 2022002942 (print)
LCCN 2022002943 (ebook)
ISBN 9781636907956 (hardcover)
ISBN 9781636907963 (paperback)
ISBN 9781636907970 (ebook)
Subjects: LCSH: Feral swine–Juvenile literature.
Introduced mammals–Juvenile literature.
Pest introduction–Juvenile literature.
Classification: LCC SF397.8 .K54 2023 (print) | LCC SF397.8 (ebook) | DDC 599.63/3–dc23/eng/20220126
LC record available at https://lccn.loc.gov/2022002942
LC ebook record available at https://lccn.loc.gov/2022002943

Editor: Eliza Leahy
Designer: Michelle Sonnek

Photo Credits: Eric Isselee/Shutterstock, cover; Victoria Wright/Shutterstock, 1; Jim Cumming/Shutterstock, 3; Goran Jakus/Shutterstock, 4; ENRIQUE ALAEZ PEREZ/Shutterstock, 5; Gary Rolband/Shutterstock, 6-7; Czesznak Zsolt/Shutterstock, 8; Ben Schonewille/Shutterstock, 9; Violetastock/iStock, 10-11; Bruce Corbett/Alamy, 12-13; OceanProd/iStock, 14-15; Stouffer Productions/Age Fotostock, 16-17; Chase D'animulls/Shutterstock, 18; Coco-rentin/Shutterstock, 19; smilesbevie/Shutterstock, 20-21; Rixipix/iStock, 23.

Printed in the United States of America at Corporate Graphics in North Mankato, Minnesota.

TABLE OF CONTENTS

CHAPTER 1

PROBLEM PIGS

A farmer checks his **crops**. Cornstalks stood tall yesterday. Today, they are on the ground. The field is torn up. What caused this?

Feral pigs are to blame. Feral pigs are wild. They are sometimes called wild boars. They are not kept as farm animals. But they can destroy farms and other areas by **rooting**.

Feral pigs live in many **habitats**. These include swamps, grasslands, forests, and mountains. They live in different **climates**, too.

DID YOU KNOW?

A feral pig can weigh as much as a lion! Males can be more than seven feet (2.1 meters) long. The pigs have long **snouts**.

snout

CHAPTER 2

SPREADING SPECIES

Feral pigs are **native** to Europe and Asia. They are an **invasive species** in North America. Explorers and **settlers** brought them in the 1500s. Since then, feral pigs have spread across North America.

They have few **predators** in their new home. Some animals, like black bears and alligators, hunt them. But it is not enough to stop the pigs. Why? The pigs **reproduce** quickly. Females often have 10 or more piglets each year!

piglets

People hunt feral pigs for sport. But this also helped the pigs spread. How? Hunters brought them to new places to start hunting areas. The pigs reproduced faster than people could hunt them.

DID YOU KNOW?

Feral pigs live in groups called sounders. A sounder can have dozens of pigs.

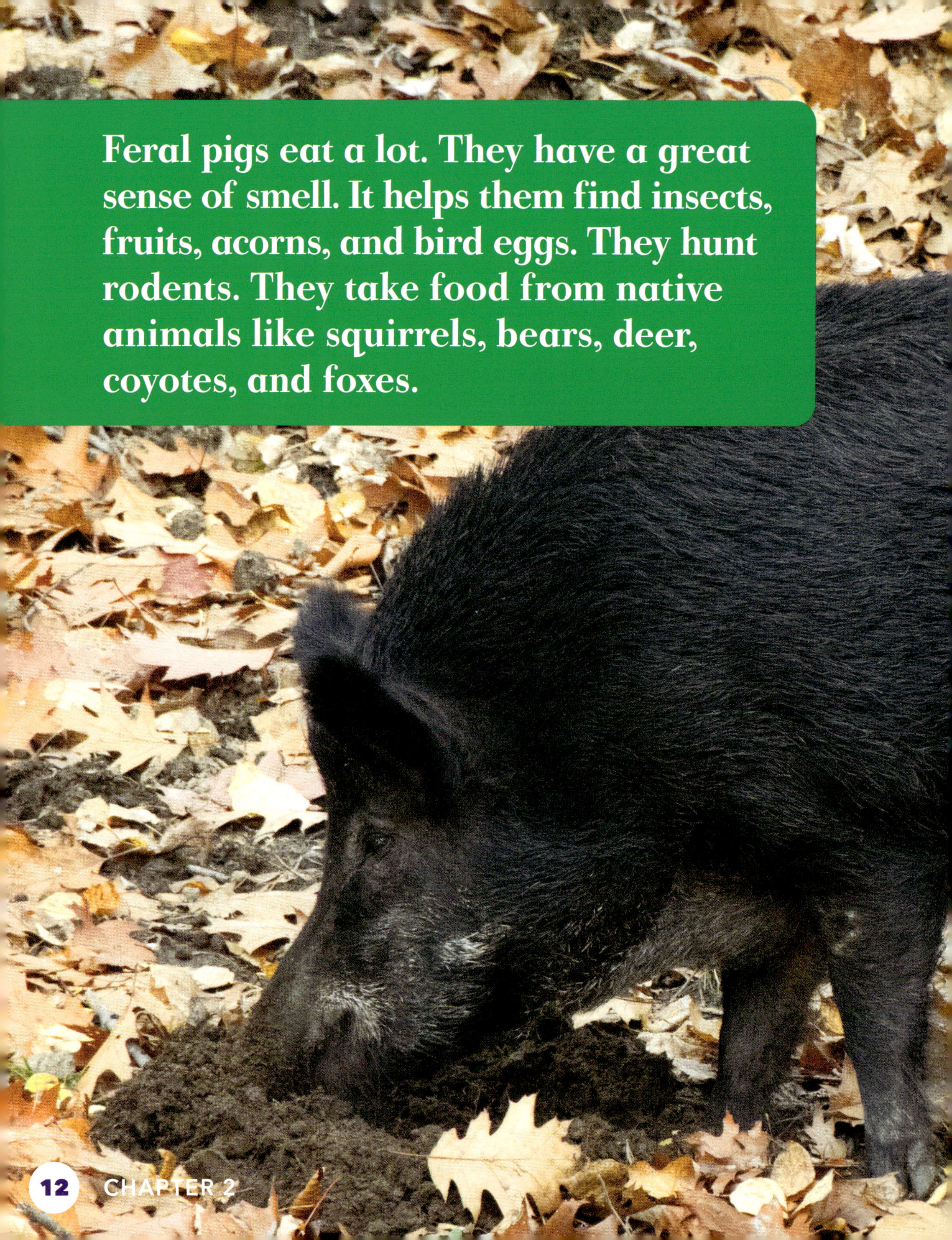

Feral pigs eat a lot. They have a great sense of smell. It helps them find insects, fruits, acorns, and bird eggs. They hunt rodents. They take food from native animals like squirrels, bears, deer, coyotes, and foxes.

TAKE A LOOK!

Feral pigs live in many parts of the United States and Canada. Take a look!

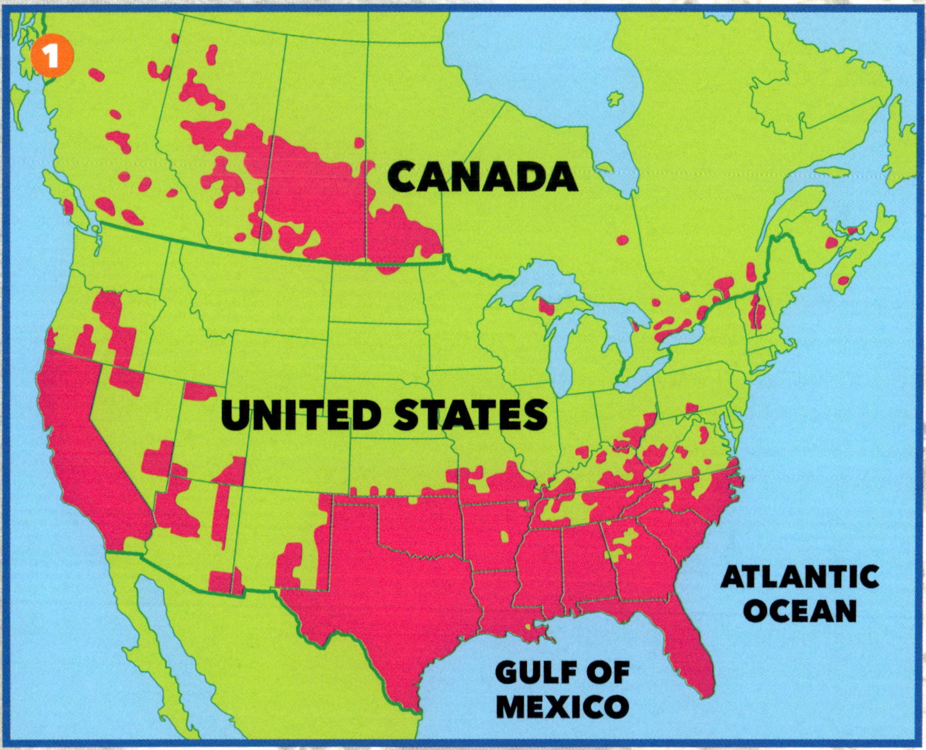

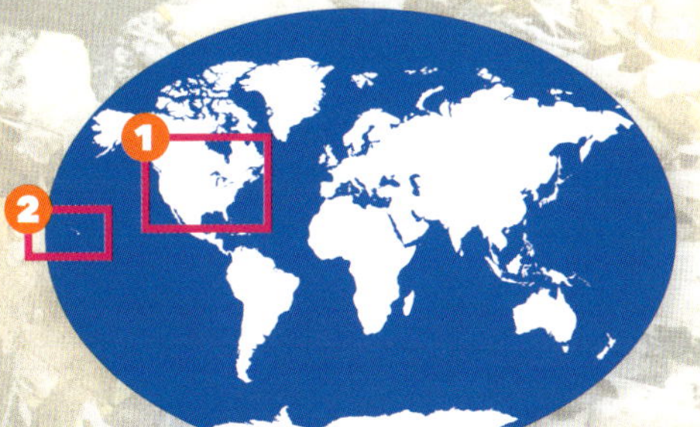

Feral pigs root for food. They use their snouts and **tusks**. They dig to find insects and plants. This causes damage. It wrecks roads and lawns. It destroys crops.

DID YOU KNOW?

Feral pigs cause billions of dollars in damage each year in the United States. Most of this cost is crop damage.

feral pig
damage

bobwhite quail nest

Rooting also harms habitats. Feral pigs tear up ground nests of birds like the bobwhite quail. They also destroy the nests of some sea turtles. They dig up milkweed. Monarch butterflies need this plant to survive.

CHAPTER 3

STOPPING THE SPREAD

People are working to stop feral pigs from spreading. But it is tough to catch them. Why? These pigs are fast. They can run up to 30 miles (48 kilometers) per hour!

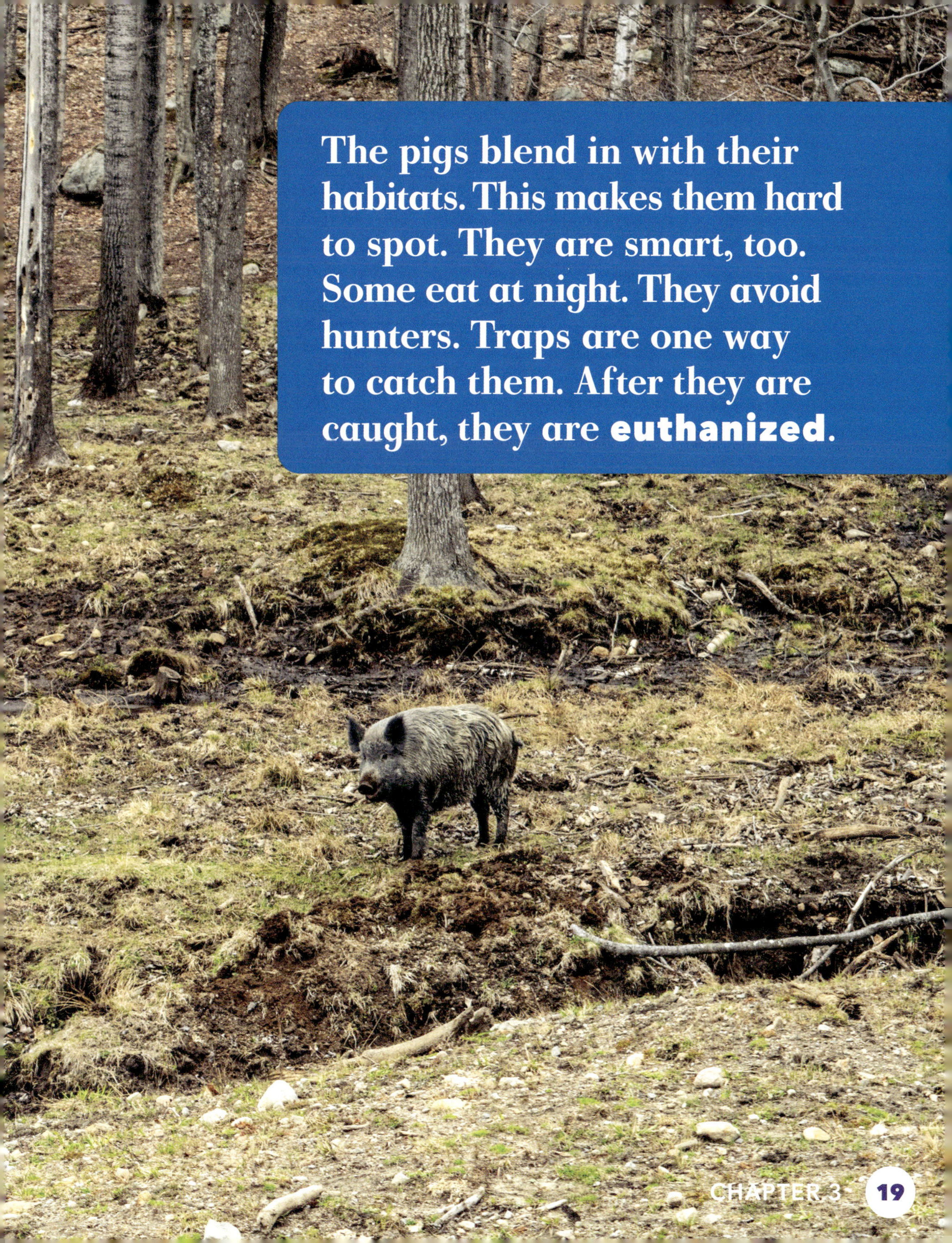

The pigs blend in with their habitats. This makes them hard to spot. They are smart, too. Some eat at night. They avoid hunters. Traps are one way to catch them. After they are caught, they are **euthanized**.

Scientists **track** feral pigs. They want to learn where these animals will go next.

North America is not the pigs' natural home. Insects and animals like monarch butterflies and bobwhite quails would be healthier without them.

monarch
butterfly

ACTIVITIES & TOOLS

TRY THIS!

SUPER SNIFFERS

Feral pigs can smell odors several miles away. This helps them find food and succeed as an invasive species. Test your sense of smell in this fun activity!

What You Need:

- five different scented food items
- teaspoon
- five small cups
- aluminum foil
- pencils
- masking tape
- marker
- sheets of paper
- a few classmates, friends, or family members

1. **Have an adult help you choose five different scented food items. Place a teaspoon or less of each in its own cup.**
2. **Cover each cup with a piece of aluminum foil. With a pencil, poke a tiny hole in the center of the foil.**
3. **Write numbers and food names on pieces of masking tape to label each cup. For example: #1 – Cinnamon. Place the labels on the bottom of each cup.**
4. **Give each person who is trying the activity a sheet of paper. Have them sniff each cup. Then, ask them to write their guesses on their paper.**
5. **Share what the correct answers were. Which person in your group was the Super Sniffer?**

GLOSSARY

climates: The weather typical of certain places over long periods of time.

crops: Plants that are grown as food.

euthanized: Put to death in a humane manner.

feral: Wild.

habitats: The places where animals or plants are usually found.

invasive species: Any kind of living organism that is not native to a specific area.

native: Growing or living naturally in a particular area of the world.

predators: Animals that hunt other animals for food.

reproduce: To produce offspring.

rooting: Turning up soil with the snout to look for food.

settlers: People who make a home or live in a new place.

snouts: The long front parts of some animals' heads that include the nose, mouth, and jaws.

track: To follow and try to find an animal by looking for marks or traces of it.

tusks: The long, curved, pointed teeth that can stick out of the mouths of animals such as feral pigs.

INDEX

TO LEARN MORE

Finding more information is as easy as 1, 2, 3.

1. Go to www.factsurfer.com
2. Enter "feralpigs" into the search box.
3. Choose your book to see a list of websites.

FACT SURFER